Green with Envy

Don't miss any of Bella
and Glimmer's adventures!

Unicorn Magic

Coming soon

Unicorn Magic

- BOOK 3 -

Green with Envy

BY JESSICA BURKHART

Illustrated by Victoria Ying

Aladdin

NEW YORK LONDON TORONTO SYDNEY NEW DELHI

This book is a work of fiction. Any references to historical events, real people,
or real places are used fictitiously. Other names, characters, places, and events
are products of the author's imagination, and any resemblance to actual
events or places or persons, living or dead, is entirely coincidental.

ALADDIN

An imprint of Simon & Schuster Children's Publishing Division
1230 Avenue of the Americas, New York, NY 10020
This Aladdin paperback edition December 2014
Text copyright © 2014 by Jessica Burkhart
Cover illustrations copyright © 2014 by Victoria Ying
Interior illustrations by Victoria Ying
All rights reserved, including the right of reproduction in whole or in part in any form.
ALADDIN is a trademark of Simon & Schuster, Inc., and related logo
is a registered trademark of Simon & Schuster, Inc.
Also available in an Aladdin hardcover edition.
For information about special discounts for bulk purchases, please contact
Simon & Schuster Special Sales at 1-866-506-1949
or business@simonandschuster.com.
The Simon & Schuster Speakers Bureau can bring authors to your live event.
For more information or to book an event contact the
Simon & Schuster Speakers Bureau at 1-866-248-3049 or
visit our website at www.simonspeakers.com.
Cover designed by Jessica Handelman
Interior designed by Mike Rosamilia
The text of this book was set in Arno Pro.
Manufactured in the United States of America 1114 OFF
2 4 6 8 10 9 7 5 3 1
Library of Congress Control Number 2014952850
ISBN 978-1-4814-1107-3 (hc)
ISBN 978-1-4424-9826-6 (pbk)
ISBN 978-1-4424-9827-3 (eBook)

Contents

1

Spilling Secrets

"Next Friday is going to be the best day *ever!*"
Princess Bella said to her two best friends. Ivy
and Clara walked beside Bella as the three girls
left their classroom on Friday afternoon. The girls
had school every day at Crystal Castle—Bella's
home—and shared the classroom with six other
third-grade students. Most of them, like Ivy, had
parents who worked at Crystal Castle. Another
student, older by a year, was Ben.

Ben had just joined Bella's class when he had
come to Crystal Castle to be an apprentice for his
uncle Frederick. Frederick was the royal stable

manager, and he had put Ben to work helping care for the castle's prized unicorns, including Bella's own unicorn, Glimmer.

Bella's closest friends weren't official "royals," but they were princesses to her!

"I know!" Ivy said. "No school for an entire week! I love spring break!" She slung her pink shimmery backpack over one shoulder. Pieces of her white-blond hair were twisted and held off her face by several rhinestone butterfly hair clips. The enchanted butterfly wings fluttered open and shut, making the gemstones sparkle.

"That's *so* exciting, but I'm with Bella," Clara said. "Friday is huge!" Clara, the most outgoing of the three friends, skipped ahead a couple of steps, then turned around and walked backward so she faced her friends. Clara's backpack, covered in teensy blue lights that flashed on when the bag moved, rolled beside her on wheels over the castle's marble floor.

Bella and Ivy giggled at Clara as she almost tripped over her own feet.

"My parents didn't even tell me that they were going to throw a party for our class," Bella said. "We get the whole week off, and on Friday is the party, with a movie in the garden, desserts, and music. And we all get to hang out."

Bella smiled at the thought of spending more time with her classmates. Lately, the princess had barely enough time to see her besties.

"Plus, there's an *extra* surprise that I didn't tell you about yet," Bella said mysteriously.

Clara stopped so suddenly that Bella and Ivy almost plowed into her.

"Spill!" Clara said, her long strawberry-blond waves swishing around her shoulders.

"Tell us!" Ivy added, making wide eyes and pouting.

Bella laughed. "Okay. Want to go to the stables? We could sit with Glimmer and talk. We already got the okay from your parents for you to stay after school for a while."

"Stables. Yes! Let's go! I want to know the extra surprise!" Clara said, grabbing the hands of Ivy and Bella and pulling them forward.

They ran, laughing, down a long hallway in the castle. The girls stopped in front of the giant wooden front door, and Clara told her backpack to "stay." Ivy put hers beside Clara's, and Bella dropped her own purple one on the pile.

A castle security guard, gleaming sword at his side, opened the door for them. Bright sunlight almost blinded Bella for a moment as she skipped with her friends across the Crystal Castle lawn toward the stable.

Bella carefully looked over the grounds. She wanted everything to be perfect for her surprise. But there wasn't a thing she would change. Royal unicorns, white as fresh snow, munched on emerald-colored grass in pastures on both sides of the castle's driveway. A few unicorns were napping—flat out on their sides—and soaking up the sun. The weather was perfect—warm but not too hot. It was Bella's favorite time of year.

The girls reached the stables and slowed to a walk so they didn't scare any of the unicorns. The royal stables had a mint-green exterior and a black roof.

Inside, a large main aisle had a row of stalls on either side. Since it was so nice out, most of the stalls were empty, as the unicorns were outside. But at the end of the left aisle, a closed stall door held one *very* special unicorn. Bella craned her neck, looking for Ben.

"Glimmer!" Bella called. "We're here!"

She couldn't help but smile when her beautiful unicorn stuck her head over the stall door. The purple tinted unicorn neighed excitedly when she saw Bella.

Bella slid the giant bolt on the stall door and opened it. Ivy and Clara followed her inside, shutting the door behind them.

"Hi, Glimmer," Bella said softly. "Pretty girl." The princess hugged Glimmer's neck while Ivy and Clara petted her.

Glimmer bumped her velvet-soft nose against Bella's hands, making the princess laugh.

Bella and Glimmer shared a very special bond. Just under a week ago, Glimmer had disappeared from the royal stables. At first Bella had been certain her unicorn had been uni-napped, until she got help from Ben, Ivy, and Clara. They learned that Glimmer had run away, and after days of searching,

Bella had found Glimmer deep in the scary Dark Forest. The princess had pleaded with Glimmer to follow her out of the dangerous woods. She wanted Glimmer to be safe, even if Glimmer didn't want to be her unicorn.

As Glimmer had nudged Bella's hands just now, it was something the unicorn had done in the woods. When Glimmer touched Bella, something magical happened between them. Bella was able to read Glimmer's body language and, almost like mind reading, be able to tell what Glimmer was thinking or how she was feeling.

That day, surrounded by the Dark Forest, Glimmer had told Bella that she was scared to be the princess's unicorn. Glimmer loved Bella more than anything, but worried she wouldn't be good enough.

Bella assured Glimmer that the unicorn was perfect and everything she wanted.

Princess Bella jumped, startled, as Glimmer bumped her hands a little harder.

"It's like Glimmer's saying, 'Earth to Bella,'" Ivy said with a smile.

"True. She's also saying, 'Get me a treat, please,'" Bella said.

She ran a hand down Glimmer's white neck with her light-purple-tinged mane. "I'll get you one before we leave, okay?"

Glimmer bobbed her head.

The girls settled onto the clean straw and Glimmer, not wanting to be left out, folded her legs under her and delicately lowered herself to the stall floor.

"Aw! I *have* to take a picture of this, even though I don't have my camera," Clara said. She made a rectangle shape with her fingers, touching her pointer fingers to her thumbs. Photos were always better with a camera, but magic worked in a pinch. "Photograph," she commanded. She closed one eye and moved her hands closer to Glimmer. "Take picture now."

Click!

A small burst of sparkles shimmered into the air. The photo appeared in the air, and Ivy and Clara tilted their heads to see it.

"Ooh!" Bella exclaimed. "Send me that picture!"

Clara nodded. "I will. Camera, I'm finished." The image of Glimmer vanished.

"So do you guys remember my cousin Violet?" Bella asked.

"She's a princess in Foris Kingdom, right?" Ivy asked. "A few months younger than us?"

Foris Kingdom was on one of four sky islands— pieces of land that floated way above the clouds. A person could only reach another island if a rainbow or moonbow was cast. Then the sky island was in walking distance.

"Right," Bella said. "Violet's dad is my uncle,

King Alexander—my dad's brother. You guys know how close Violet and I are. Even though she lives in Foris, we've been like best friends since we could walk."

"You've talked a lot about her," Clara said. "She sounds so nice."

Bella smiled. "She is. We've bonded even more since my Pair to Glimmer."

"That makes sense," Ivy said. "Did Violet want to know all about your Pairing? I know I would."

Bella nodded. "I told her most of it over the phone." She sighed. "I really wish you could meet her."

Ivy and Clara both frowned, sticking out their bottom lips.

"We would have so much fun together," Bella said. "And we will because . . . Violet's coming to visit! Surprise!"

2

Two Princesses + One Celebration = Awesome!

"BELLA!" Ivy and Clara shrieked.

Bella giggled at her friends' faces. They were pink from shouting, and even Glimmer looked as if she was almost smiling.

"You sneak!" Ivy said. "When is she coming?"

"Tomorrow!" Bella said. "Violet's staying at the castle all week, and she's coming to our class party on Friday."

"Ooh, yay!" Clara said. She clasped her hands together.

"My mom, dad, and I are meeting her at the

end of the rainbow from the Foris Kingdom exit,"
Bella said.

"Just when I thought next week couldn't get any
better," Ivy said. She twirled a stalk of straw around
her finger. "I can't wait for Violet to get here."

Glimmer added a soft whicker as if stating her
opinion.

"This is going to be so much fun! You said you

told Violet about your Pairing Ceremony," Clara said. "Have you talked about auras yet? Does Violet know about Queen Fire?"

Bella shook her head. "Not yet. I told Violet the basics: that the aura appears on your eighth birthday. When the aura appears, you get to walk down a line of royal unicorns, watching each unicorn glow a different color until you both have the same aura glow color. I told Violet that mine is purple and, of course, sent her a million photos of Glimmer, but I haven't told her about Queen Fire."

Just saying the words "Queen Fire" left a bad taste in Bella's mouth.

"Are you going to tell her?" Ivy asked, her voice soft.

It hadn't been even a week since Bella had been up against the evil queen who ruled the Blacklands—a dangerous place that no one went near—and the Dark Forest.

"I think I have to," Bella said. "Violet is family. Queen Fire is my"—she swallowed—"my mom's twin sister. My aunt. I don't want to keep a secret that big from her."

Bella shook her head hard, trying to send thoughts of Queen Fire away. She knew she had to tell Violet—her younger cousin was three weeks away from her own Pairing Ceremony.

"No more talk of You Know Who today," Clara declared. "We have lots of things to be excited about."

Bella smiled. "We so do! A sleepover is a must this week. I want you both here as much as possible all week long."

Just the thought of Violet visiting made Bella want to do cartwheels. Violet was one of her best friends, and they hadn't had a week together in years. Usually they only saw each other during holidays or vacations. They had *so* much to talk about!

Violet's parents had agreed to let the princess have a week off from her private tutor to spend time at Crystal Castle. Bella's dad, King Phillip, had assured Violet's parents that his niece needed to come spend time with kids her own age and the party would be good for her. The king and queen hadn't wanted Bella to grow up lonely or without interaction with kids her own age, so that was why they had decided to have a small classroom in Crystal Castle.

"Did I mention how *amazing* this week is going to be?" Bella asked. She grinned, and they all cracked up. Laughing, the three friends high-fived.

3

Instant Besties

"Mom! Dad! We're going to be late!" Bella called up the winding staircase. She shook her head, sending her wavy brown hair across her shoulders.

"Bells, don't worry," Lyssa said. "You'll make it in plenty of time to pick up Violet."

Lyssa was Bella's handmaiden. But that sounded like a stuffy title.

Lyssa, who was fourteen years old, was really more like an older sister. Since last year, Lyssa had helped Bella with getting dressed, doing home-work, and, today, carefully curling Bella's straight brown hair into waves.

"Are you sure?" Bella asked. "What if the Rainbow Rail Express gets here early?"

The Rainbow Rail Express was a fairly new mode of transportation. It allowed passengers to travel to the other sky islands. Each morning someone important at the station had to cast a spell to connect one island to the next. Rainbow Rail was so new that even Bella hadn't been on it yet.

Lyssa smiled. "If it does, I'm sure Violet will call or message you."

Bella walked away from the staircase. "Mirror," she said, snapping her fingers.

A mirror appeared in front of Bella. The princess eyed her hair and clothes. Lyssa, who usually took weekends off, had come to Crystal Castle this morning to help Bella get ready for Violet's arrival.

"Do you think this dress is right, Lys?" Bella asked. The princess scanned her reflection in the mirror. The sleeveless soft-pink dress had a full tulle skirt and a rosette at the waist. Bella turned and looked over her shoulder. A satin tie was looped in a pretty bow at the back, which buttoned up.

"I think it's *perfect*," Lyssa said. "You tried on four other dresses before deciding on this one, remember?" The older girl walked over to Bella and hugged her.

Bella squeezed Lyssa back, glad that she had Lyssa's help to choose today's outfit. "I'm so nervous!" Bella admitted. "Isn't that silly?"

She walked over to a red velvet-covered bench and sat down. Lyssa sat beside her, turning so she faced Bella.

"It's not silly at all," Lyssa said. She tucked a strand of shoulder-length honey-blond hair behind her ear. Her green eyes were kind as she looked at Bella.

"It *feels* silly," Bella said. "Violet's my cousin.

18

We talk all of the time. I want to make this week the best for her. I don't want Violet wishing she had stayed home."

"Hosting a houseguest makes *anyone* nervous," Lyssa said. "You're a little scared because you care so much. Like you said, you want to make this visit great for Violet. If you didn't care, you wouldn't be nervous."

"Really?" Bella looked up at Lyssa. The older girl somehow always knew what to say to make Bella feel better.

Lyssa nodded. "Really. I bet Violet's nervous too. She probably wants to be a good guest and not make *you* wish she had stayed in Foris."

"Never!" Bella said. "I wish she could stay here forever."

Lyssa and Bella laughed, and the prickles of nerves evaporated from Bella's body.

There was the sound of footsteps on the stairs,

and King Phillip and Queen Katherine descended the staircase.

"Thank you, Lys," Bella said, hugging the girl again.

"Anytime! Have fun!" Lyssa said. They stood and Lyssa dipped her head as the king and queen approached, before she exited the room.

"Ready to go, Bells?" King Phillip, smiling, looked down at his daughter. Queen Katherine, in a flowing hunter-green dress, stood next to him.

"Yes! Yes!" Bella exclaimed. "Let's go!"

The guards opened the doors, and the royal family stepped outside and headed for the Royal Carriage. The giant orb-shaped carriage extended stairs and opened its doors so Bella and her parents could climb inside.

The Royal Carriage was solar powered and required no driver. King Phillip and Queen Katherine were the only voices the Royal Carriage listened to for directions. Bella settled herself on the cushy seat across from her parents.

"Please take us to the Rainbow Rail Station at the Foris Kingdom platform," King Phillip commanded the carriage. "At the fastest speed."

Without hesitation, the carriage glided forward. It moved over the gravel driveway and passed the guards who stood like statues on either side of the drawbridge. The guards' armor had the Crystal Kingdom seal: a diamond with two rearing unicorns below. The words CRYSTAL KINGDOM ran under the unicorns.

The carriage turned onto the road and then zipped through the countryside toward the Rainbow Rail Station. Trees, fields, and houses whizzed by. "What are you going to do first with Violet?" Queen Katherine asked Bella.

"Introduce her to Glimmer," Bella said. "I can't wait for them to meet!"

She had barely finished her sentence when the carriage started to slow. Rainbow Rail Station came into view. The station—with signs pointing to different rails to various sky islands and kingdoms—wasn't crowded. A line of five or six people, suitcases trailing behind them, walked away from the platform as one of the silver bullet-shaped trains left the station. It was daylight, so the train followed rainbow paths. When night arrived, moonbows would be cast to take over.

Bella followed her parents out of the carriage. Together, they walked to a concrete platform with a sign above that flashed FORIS. DEPARTURES AND ARRIVALS. As they walked, people who caught their eye bowed their heads or smiled at the royal family. No one snapped photos or gawked. King Phillip and Queen Katherine had worked very hard to make sure their family was approachable and normal— just like every other resident in Crystal Kingdom.

"Violet's train should be arriving at noon," Queen Katherine said. "The schedule says it's on time. See?" The queen pointed to a large board above the platform. It listed all the current train schedules and whether or not a train was delayed. A clock next to the board read 11:59 a.m. Violet would be in Crystal Kingdom any second!

Bella craned her neck and stood on tiptoes, looking down the rainbow for the train. She blinked and a silver train, sunlight glinting off the roof, raced toward the platform.

"Mom! Dad!" Bella said, hopping up and down. "She's here! That's Violet's train!" The speeding train halted silently, and the doors slid open at the front of the train. A handful of people were now standing around the royal family as if they were waiting for someone too. Bella tried to look inside the train through its windows to see if she could spot Violet, but there were too many people moving around. A line of people began exiting the train and spilling onto the platform.

"Do you see her?" Bella asked her dad.

"Not yet," King Phillip said. "Stay still and let Violet find us."

Bella's view of the train exit was blocked as a group of people stopped and gazed around. Where was Violet?

"Uncle Phillip! Aunt Katherine!"

A small figure pushed through the crowd and stopped, grinning, in front of the princess and her parents.

"Violet!" Bella said. "You made it!"

All of Bella's earlier nerves disappeared the second she saw her cousin. Violet dashed toward Bella, her long red curls bouncing, and they hugged. Violet's powder-blue dress looked pretty against her red hair, and she had on silver ballet flats that were almost identical to Bella's.

"Violet, darling, you look beautiful!" Queen Katherine said. She wrapped her arms around Violet, and King Phillip was next in line for a hug.

"I'm *so* happy to be here," Violet said. Her hazel eyes sparkled with excitement. "I was practically counting the seconds on the train ride."

"Let's get off the platform and start the journey home," King Phillip said. He snapped his fingers at Violet's sparkly suitcase. "This way, ladies."

Bella's dad helped his wife, daughter, and niece maneuver through the crowd. The townspeople respectfully stepped aside to allow the royal family to exit. The king and queen got a few paces ahead. Violet grabbed Bella's hand, and the girls grinned at each other. They skipped forward but slowed when they couldn't get by a family that was shuffling along, their luggage floating alongside them.

"*Excuse* me!" Violet said with a huff, then rolled her eyes.

Violet pulled on Bella's hand, pushing them past the group. Bella looked back over her shoulder as the family frowned and watched them walk away, whispering to each other. The princess's face turned bright pink. *That was so rude!* Bella thought. Violet had never done anything like that before.

"Vi," Bella said. "They had a lot of stuff—"

Violet sighed. "I know. I haven't slept much lately! I've been too excited and I guess I'm kind of cranky."

That made sense. Bella smiled at her cousin and kept going toward the carriage.

Once they reached the carriage, everyone settled in, and King Phillip requested that it take them home.

Bella, sitting across from Violet, caught her cousin's eye. There were a few moments of silence. "Omigosh—" Violet started.

"We have—" Bella said at the same time.

They burst into giggles.

"You go," Bella said.

"No, you go!" Violet said.

"Oh, girls. Come on now," Queen Katherine said. "Don't you have anything to talk about? Why all the silence?"

Everyone in the carriage laughed.

"I've been counting the days until you got here," Bella told her cousin. "I was going a little crazy this morning. It felt like noon was never going to come!"

Violet nodded. "I know! I felt the same way. On the train, I asked the conductor *twice* if we were going to arrive on time, because I was sure the train was moving too slow."

"You're here now, and that's all that matters. I have the *best* week planned." Bella smiled. "Friday is going to be so much fun. You'll get to meet everyone in my class."

"I can't wait. But I'm dying to meet Glimmer," Violet said. "I feel like I know her already after everything you've told me."

"She's so excited to meet you, too," Bella agreed. The carriage pulled away from the station and headed home to Crystal Castle.

Bella and Violet chatted the entire way home. They didn't stop as the carriage glided back across the drawbridge and approached the castle. Violet had seen Crystal Castle before. Her attention was on something else: the unicorns.

"Look at them!" Violet pointed, climbing out of the carriage. She shielded her eyes with a hand and looked toward the pastures dotted with grazing unicorns.

"Violet," Queen Katherine said. "Are you tired from traveling? Or hungry? You can come inside and rest for a while if you would like."

"Thank you, Aunt Katherine," Violet said. "But I'm way too excited to be tired! Can Bella show me Glimmer?"

"Please?" Bella added.

"Go have fun," Bella's mom said, smiling.

"Come on! This way!" Bella grabbed Violet's hand. Giggling, they ran to the stable, and skidded to a stop when they reached the entrance.

"Frederick is the stable manager," Bella said. "Don't run in the stable unless you want to get in trouble."

Violet nodded, eyes wide.

As they moved closer, Bella could see a unicorn tied to a stall. But it wasn't just *any* unicorn.

"There she is," Bella said, looking at Violet. "That's Glimmer!"

Someone walked around Glimmer's far side, brush in hand.

"Ben, hi," Bella said.

Ben smiled and waved the brush as the girls walked down the stable aisle.

"Ben is Frederick's nephew," Bella explained to Violet. "He's from Foris too. He goes to school with my friends and me and works at the stable before and after class."

They reached Ben, and Violet shyly shook his hand. "I think every other word I've heard for a week has been 'Violet,'" Ben said, then laughed. "Bella, I hope you don't mind. I took Glimmer out to groom her so she'd be extra shiny for company."

"Mind? Not at all! Thank you," Bella said.

Glimmer wore a lavender-purple headpiece attached to a matching rope so Bella or Ben could lead her. Ben stepped away from Glimmer and stood next to Bella. The unicorn turned her head, looked at Violet, and let out a snort.

"She's saying hi," Bella said. "What do you think?"

Violet didn't move or speak. She just blinked for several seconds.

"She's *beautiful*," Violet finally said. Bella wasn't going to disagree. Every inch of Glimmer's coat sparkled like fresh snow. Her purple-tinged mane and tail were combed straight. Glimmer strained against her rope to reach her muzzle closer to Violet.

Violet's eyes shifted to Bella's.

"It's okay," Bella said. "Glimmer's so friendly. She wouldn't hurt anyone."

Violet took a tiny step forward, and Glimmer slowly lowered her muzzle into Violet's open hands. The princess of Foris laughed.

"Her whiskers are tickly," Violet said. She ran a hand up Glimmer's forehead and petted her cheek. "Wow. She is so soft!"

Glimmer blinked her big brown eyes and leaned into Violet's hand. Bella couldn't help the grin spreading across her face. Her favorite cousin and her favorite unicorn had already become friends.

"I've never seen Glimmer so friendly with anyone new," Ben said. He folded his arms, smiling. "She really likes you, Violet."

Bella's cousin grinned. "I *really* like her. She's perfect, Bella."

Bella reached up and scratched behind Glimmer's left ear. "I know she is. You're going to have so much fun with her all week."

"Can I brush her?" Violet asked. She looked from Ben to Bella.

"Sure," Bella said. "She loves it."

"I'll show you how," Ben said, handing Violet the blue-bristled brush he held. "But be careful of your toes." He picked up another brush and nodded toward Violet's ballet flats.

"We will both wear boots next time," Bella said. "Violet was so excited to meet Glimmer that we came straight from the carriage."

"Bella said you're from Foris," Violet said to Ben. She mimicked him as he stepped up to Glimmer's side and flicked the brush lightly over the unicorn's coat.

"My family is still there," Ben said. "Except for my uncle. He is allowing me to be his apprentice and learn everything about unicorns."

Glimmer blinked slowly and peeked through her big eyelashes. Bella knew that look well. The princess leaned against the stall door.

"You guys are spoiling Glimmer," Bella said in a teasing tone. "She has not one but two grooms. Glimmer's so relaxed she's starting to fall asleep."

Violet threw her arms around Glimmer's neck and hugged the unicorn. "Get your beauty sleep, Glimmer."

Something pulsed inside the right pocket of Bella's dress. She pulled out her Chat Crystal—a quarter-size stone. The stone changed colors and vibrated depending on who contacted Bella. She had cast a spell on the stone to become a vibrant purple when Queen Katherine messaged her.

"It's from my mom," Bella explained, letting the crystal lie flat on her palm. "We better go up to the castle, Violet."

"Oh, fine," Violet sighed, sticking out her bottom lip. "We will come back, right?"

"Only all the time!" Bella said. "We can visit Glimmer after dinner, I bet."

Violet smiled and slid her arms around Glimmer's neck. She squeezed the unicorn tight, and Glimmer leaned into the hug. "I don't know how you ever leave her," Violet said.

Bella stood on her tiptoes and kissed Glimmer's cheek. "I'm only able to leave because I know I can come right back," she replied.

The girls said good-bye to Ben, Violet gave Glimmer a final hug, and the girls left the stable.

"Aren't you *so* excited that you'll have a unicorn just like Glimmer soon?" Bella asked.

Violet nodded. "I can't wait. Glimmer is *so* special—you're lucky, Bella. I want to spend the whole break in the stable!"

"We can do that," Bella said. "But it's even better with Clara and Ivy—my best friends that I've told you about."

"Meeting Glimmer and now your friends—yay!" Violet said. She looped an arm through Bella's. "This is going to be the best vacation ever!"

"It so is!" Bella agreed. "And speaking of Glimmer, I am *so* excited to tell you all about my Pairing Ceremony! It's going to be so much better in person than over Chat Crystals."

"Yeah, me too," Violet said slowly. She looked over at Bella. "Race you!" Violet tore off toward the castle, laughing as she ran. Bella sprinted after her, giggling so hard she could barely walk.

4

Early Princess Gets the Unicorn

Bright sunlight filled Bella's room. She blinked slowly and yawned, stretching in her bed. *I love Saturdays,* she thought. *And Violet's asleep just down the hall!* That made Saturday even better.

On the wall at the end of Bella's bed, a handful of sparkly silver letters read HAPPY WEEKEND! They were Blinkers, and using her voice, Bella was able to change their color and message anytime she wanted. The Blinkers knew her so well that they had already preprogrammed their "Happy Weekend" message to appear every Saturday.

Yesterday Bella had helped Violet unpack and

settle into her guest room. One of the maids hung all of Violet's clothes in the closet. The girls picked out a pair of Bella's riding boots for Violet so her toes would be safe from unicorn hooves.

They'd ended up sitting cross-legged across from each other, talking and swapping stories until Queen Katherine called them for dinner. Bella had asked Violet if she wanted to talk about the Pairing Ceremony, but Violet was too sleepy. She said she wanted to be super awake when she heard the story. Bella's mom wanted to end the night with the family all together, so she and King Phillip had watched a movie with Bella and Violet until bedtime.

After such a full day, and with all of the excitement with Violet's arrival, Bella had fallen asleep as soon as her head hit the pillow.

Bella rolled over onto her side and checked the time on her pink alarm clock. It was barely after eight. *Violet has to be tired from traveling,* Bella thought. *I want to wake her up to hang out with me, but that would be mean. I can wait a little longer.*

Bella sat up, stretching her arms. She slid out from under her covers and plucked a cozy cotton robe off her closet door. The princess went to her favorite spot in the entire castle—her window seat.

She watched the flowers wake up—yawning and stretching like the princess had done moments earlier. Unicorns nibbled at the grass in pastures surrounding the castle. A handful of people whose faces Bella couldn't make out unloaded wood from a large van. Bella followed the workers with her eyes and realized what they were building: a *stage.* What would a stage—?

"Oh!" Bella said. She put her nose against the windowpane. The stage was for Friday's party!

Queen Katherine had mentioned to her last week that workers would be making an outdoor dance floor. Bella had been excited at the time but forgot about it as her cousin's visit got closer and closer.

I didn't even get to explain the class party to Violet last night, Bella thought. Both princesses had gone straight to bed after the movie. King Phillip almost had to carry sleepy Violet up the stairs.

Bella couldn't wait another second. Violet had to see this! The princess hopped off her window seat and sprinted across her room. She lifted a foot, and one of her slippers—purple with pink sequins—lifted off the floor and glided onto her foot. Bella opened her bedroom door and hurried down the hallway. She eased open the door to the guest room.

The large four-poster bed was empty. The bed had been made up with a daisy-patterned quilt, and the blinds were open.

"Violet?" Bella called out, walking into the bedroom. The bathroom door on the right side of the room was open, and no one was inside.

Bella left the guest room and headed down the hallway. She hurried down a black-and-white marble spiral staircase and heard her mom's laugh coming from the kitchen. Bella pushed open the white double doors, and Queen Katherine, sipping something steaming from a mug, smiled when she saw her daughter. Thomas, the chef at Crystal Castle, stood across the kitchen island from the queen and had a pen in hand.

"Morning, sleepyhead," Queen Katherine said.

"Hi, Mom," Bella said. "Good morning, Thomas."

The black-haired chef tipped his head. "Princess Bella."

"Honey," Queen Katherine said, "Thomas

and I are putting together a menu for Friday's party. Do you want to help us with food and drink ideas?"

"Yay! That's exciting!" Bella said. "I'd love to help. But where's Violet? Her room is empty."

The queen put down her mug and waved a hand at a glass pitcher of OJ. The pitcher rose into the air, tipped, and poured orange juice into a short glass. Bella's mom handed it to Bella.

"Violet was up a couple of hours ago," Queen Katherine said. "Thomas made her a lovely breakfast, and we talked for a while."

"Oh, okay," Bella said. She took a gulp of OJ. "Where's Violet now? I have to find her and show her the view from my window. The platform for the party looks so amazing."

Queen Katherine smiled. "I'm glad you think so. Violet headed down to the stables about an hour ago. She talked about Glimmer so much,

Bella. You must be so excited that Violet and your unicorn get along so well."

Bella smiled, nodding. But *something* felt wrong.

"I wonder why Violet didn't wake me up," Bella asked.

"I'm sure she didn't want to disturb you so early in the morning," her mom said. "Have some breakfast, then change and go join her."

"I'm not that hungry," Bella said. "I'll eat a little later."

Before Queen Katherine could question why Bella was skipping breakfast—something she *never* did—Bella walked out of the kitchen and slowly climbed the stairs.

Violet and I have always woken the other person up if we were having a sleepover, Bella thought. *We never wanted to waste any time we could be spending together.*

Once she got to her room, the princess closed her door. She opened her closet door, flipped on the chandelier, and walked inside.

A nagging feeling in her stomach wouldn't go away. Why hadn't Violet asked her if they could go see Glimmer? Did Violet like *Glimmer* more than Bella? That would explain why she hadn't woken up Bella *and* why she'd gotten up so early.

Stop being silly, Bella told herself. *Violet probably wants to be around a newly matched unicorn, since she's having her own ceremony soon.*

Still feeling a little grumpy, Bella changed out of her pj's and into a sky-blue T-shirt with a sequin pocket, black leggings, and riding boots.

She sat down on her bed and dialed Clara's and Ivy's phone numbers on the castle phone in her room. "Leave message," Bella said aloud.

A small, square silver frame appeared in the air. It floated until it found the perfect spot in front of

Bella. A red light started flashing—it was time to record a message.

"Hi!" Bella said. "I wanted to see if you guys wanted to come over and meet Violet and hang out. One of our carriages can pick up both of you whenever you're ready. I'm heading down to the stable, so I'll take my Chat Crystal. Clara, send a pink signal for 'yes' and when you're on your way. Use red for 'no.' Ivy, message me with purple if you can come and blue if you can't. Bye!"

The square folded and disappeared into the air. Bella hopped off her bed, shook out her arms, and rolled her shoulders, trying to shake off her weird mood. She pocketed her Chat Crystal and left the castle.

The sun warmed Bella as she headed to the stable. The closer she got, the worse she felt about how she had reacted to Violet being at the stable. When the princess walked through the stable entrance, she was smiling as she headed for Glimmer's stall.

"Good morning, Princess Bella," Frederick said. The stable manager was fixing a gold nameplate on one of the stall doors.

"Morning," Bella said. "I hope Glimmer was a good girl last night." She stopped near a stall door and peeked inside at one of the royal unicorns.

"Perfect as always," Frederick said.

That made Bella grin.

"But if you're looking for her," Frederick said, "she's not in her stall. Ben took her out for a walk with Princess Violet."

That feeling came back deep in Bella's stomach.

"Oh," she said. "Um, okay. I'll go find them. Thank you."

She turned around and walked out of the stable. Bella walked over to the dark-brown fence that made up the riding arena. She climbed the fence and sat on the top board. Glimmer, Violet, and Ben were nowhere in sight.

I've never cared if Ben took Glimmer out of her stall, Bella thought. *I wouldn't even mind if he rode Glimmer, even though he's not allowed because she's matched to me.*

Bella didn't know why, but she was annoyed that Glimmer wasn't in her stall. It kind of felt like Violet had taken something of Bella's without asking first. Bella sighed. She knew she was being silly, but she couldn't stop how she felt. She wasn't mad at Ben, but she was irritated with Violet. *The walk was probably Violet's idea,* Bella thought. *She put Ben on the spot. He probably felt like he couldn't say no to a princess.*

Bella's shirt pocket vibrated. She reached inside and pulled out her Chat Crystal. It flashed two colors: pink and purple.

The princess let out a tiny sigh of relief. Ivy

and Clara were coming. Having her friends around would get Bella out of her bad mood.

Just relax for a minute, she thought. *It's not like Violet took Glimmer out alone. That* would *be a reason to get mad.*

Bella tipped her face toward the cloudless sky of Crystal Kingdom. She closed her eyes and took a deep breath in through her nose and a slow exhale out through her mouth. It was something her mom did to relax, and she had shown Bella. The princess took a couple of deep breaths and listened to the tweeting birds, chattering squirrels, and occasional neighs from unicorns talking to each other.

"It's just *so* crazy that you're from Foris! We have lots to talk about."

Bella opened her eyes at the sound of Violet's voice. Her cousin, Ben, and Glimmer headed her way. Ben waved with his free hand—the other held a rainbow rope attached to Glimmer.

"Good morning, Bells!" Violet said. She climbed the fence boards and sat next to Bella.

"You got up really, really early," Bella said. "I went to look for you, and my mom said you had left way before I came downstairs." She gently elbowed her cousin. "Why didn't you wake me?"

"Yeah, Vi," Ben said.

Vi? Bella thought. It had always been *Bella's* nickname for her cousin.

"I didn't want to wake you," Violet explained. "I peeked into your room before I went to breakfast. You were snoring so loud—it sounded like you really needed sleep!"

Ben grinned, looking from Violet to Bella.

Bella felt herself blush. She looked down and stuck out her hands to rub Glimmer's nose. The unicorn walked right up to Bella and thrust her nose into the princess's hands.

"Aww," Violet said, scooting closer to Bella.

"You're blushing. I didn't mean to embarrass you! You snore supercute!"

Bella nodded. "I know!" she finally said with a smile. It was no big deal. Violet didn't have an ounce of meanness in her. She wasn't making fun—right?

Glimmer moved her head out of Bella's hands and craned her neck toward Violet. The unicorn nudged Violet's arm. She squealed, hopped off the fence, and threw her arms around Glimmer.

"You're the cutest! Lucky you, Glimmer. You've got the best match in all of the kingdoms."

Bella smiled at the compliment.

"I hope it's okay that I asked Ben if we could take Glimmer for a walk," Violet said.

"Oh, um . . ." Bella stumbled over her words. "Of course."

Violet looked up at her cousin. "Are you okay? Is that a problem?"

Bella shifted her eyes from Violet to Ben to

Glimmer, then smiled. "Of course not! I'm really happy that Glimmer likes you so much."

The second part of that is true, Bella thought. *But the first kind of isn't.*

"Once Ivy and Clara get here," she said, "do you want to talk about the Pairing Ceremony?"

"Um . . ." Violet's eyes were on the driveway. She hesitated, then looked at Bella. "Maybe later, if that's cool? I'd really just love to hang out with you and your friends."

"Okay, sure," Bella said.

Suddenly a carriage appeared at the driveway of the stable. The doors opened, and Ivy and Clara climbed out. They stopped, looking in different directions for Bella. The princess wanted to shout at them, but she didn't want to scare Glimmer. Ivy spotted Ben, Violet, Glimmer, and Bella, and tapped Clara's shoulder. Both girls waved and hurried toward Bella.

"Hi, Violet!" Clara said when she and Ivy reached Bella and the others. "Finally! You're here!"

Clara gave Violet a huge hug before the princess could even introduce her cousin.

"Welcome to Crystal Kingdom!" Ivy said, hugging Violet next. "I'm Ivy, and this is Clara. We've heard *so* much about you from Bella. It's so great that you're here!"

Violet's fair cheeks flushed. "I'm so happy to meet both of *you*! Bella has told me tons of stories about her best friends."

"I didn't even get to tell you more about the party," Bella interrupted. *Ivy and Clara didn't even say hi to me,* she thought. The princess had thought that bringing Ivy and Clara over would improve her mood. Instead she felt even grumpier.

"Oh my gosh," Ivy said. "Bella! Total fail in the hosting department!"

Everyone laughed. Except Bella.

"We can tell you *everything*," Clara said. "You don't even know about the class sleepover." She clasped her hands together, grinning. "Bells, would you like to do the honors and start telling Violet about the party?"

Bella placed a hand over her stomach. She hadn't planned it, but she needed a break from everyone—even though Ivy and Clara had just arrived. "Um, actually, I'm not feeling very well."

"What's wrong?" Ben asked, his eyes darting back and forth as he looked at Bella and the rest of the girls.

"Nothing major—my stomach is just a little upset. I think I need to go back to the castle and lie down," Bella said.

The princess climbed down from the fence, and Clara put an arm across Bella's shoulders.

"I've got Glimmer," Ben said. "I'll take her back to her stall. Feel better, Bella."

Bella thought she saw a look of annoyance flicker across Violet's face.

Ivy tipped her head in the direction of the castle. "Can you walk? Or do you need to sit down somewhere softer than the fence?"

"You can sit on my jacket," Clara said. She started to shrug out of her dark jean jacket.

"Oh, no!" Bella said. "Thank you, Ivy. That's so sweet, but I can walk. And I want you guys to stay here and have fun in the stable. I'm just going to be lying down and watching TV."

"As long as you're *sure* you're okay," Violet said, "I'd like to hang out at the stable. Plus, it would be awesome to get to know you guys." She looked at Clara and Ivy. "We don't want to bother Bella if she wanted to take a nap or something."

"True . . . ," Clara said. She scrunched her eyebrows together like she always did when she was worried.

"What if we at least walk you back to the castle?" Ivy asked. "Then we'll have our Chat Crystals and we'll be there in two seconds if you message us."

"That's more than enough, guys. Thank you," Bella said. "And I'm okay to walk by myself."

Before her friends could argue any more, Bella gave them a little wave and walked away from the group.

She felt guilty *and* a little sad at the same time. She had never lied to her friends before. She had already lied to Violet about not caring that the Foris princess took Glimmer for a walk. Now Bella had just lied again to Ivy and Clara when she had told them she wanted them to stay behind.

With every step, Bella actually started to *really* feel sick. She had been sure that Violet would come back to the castle with her. Once, Bella had gotten a stomach bug during a spring vacation while her family was visiting Violet and her family.

Violet had refused to stay away from Bella, even though she could have gotten sick too. She helped the kitchen staff bring Bella chicken noodle soup, crackers, and bubbly water.

I have to remember that Vi doesn't have friends like I do, Bella thought. She took in a deep breath, trying to fight back tears. She wished Clara and Ivy wouldn't have stayed back with Violet, but the princess didn't want her friends hanging with her if they didn't want to.

The princess had also guessed that based on how fast Ivy and Clara had bonded with Violet, they, too, would stay behind.

One minute, Violet was the cousin that Bella loved and adored. The cousin that Bella was happy to share Glimmer with. The cousin that she wanted Ivy and Clara to love.

So why did these little flickers of New Violet keep coming up?

*   *   *

A couple of hours later, Bella woke up on the living room couch. She'd actually fallen asleep not too long after she'd curled herself in a blanket. She blinked, and her cousin and two besties were sitting on the floor in front of her. The girls were surrounded by shopping bags. Bags of every color and shape stretched from the fireplace to the couch.

"How are you feeling?" Violet asked.

"What is all this?" Bella asked at the same time.

"You go," Violet said.

"I feel totally fine," Bella said. "I guess I just needed a nap!"

Queen Katherine walked through the living room toward the kitchen. "How do you feel, sweetie?"

"Perfect, Mom," Bella said.

"Well, I came over to check on you and you looked so peaceful. I cast a sweet dreams spell, so

I hope you had good dreams," Queen Katherine said.

"Mom!" Bella said, yanking up the blanket to cover her face. "Sweet dreams spells are for little kids."

She started giggling, and so did Violet and her friends.

The queen blew Bella a kiss, started laughing, and walked out of the living room.

"So, where did all of this come from? What's inside the bags?" Bella asked, sitting up and stretching.

In the moments before she had fallen asleep, she had thought through everything that had just happened. Bella knew she had to keep reminding herself that her cousin didn't have a unicorn and she didn't have friends like Ivy and Clara.

Plus, knowing Ivy and Clara, they had probably thought they needed to sort of chaperone

Violet, since she was company and Bella was too sick. Bella didn't want to spend another second thinking about what had happened earlier. She was ready for a fresh start with Violet. She owed it to her cousin to give her another chance. Now, she was just excited to be with Violet and her friends.

"We were hanging out at the stable," Clara said. "I was talking to Ivy about the Crystal Kingdom Magic Market, and we both needed new outfits and sparkly jewels for the party. We had heard about a sale. Plus, Violet had never been to our amazing market!"

"You guys went to the market?" Bella asked slowly. Her friends and cousin had gone shopping? Without her?

"We called your mom to ask permission and to see if you were awake," Ivy said. "But Queen Katherine told us that you were still asleep."

"I mean, I'm glad you were able to go," Bella said. "But couldn't you guys have waited until tomorrow so we all could have gone together?"

Clara made an apologetic face. "Sorry, Bells, but there was something I really wanted for the party, and I wanted to make sure it was still there. You really didn't miss anything, so don't feel bad! I bet we can even go back tomorrow if we want."

Bella didn't even want to hear the word "shop." Violet was not making a fresh start very easy!

"Want to go to my room and watch TV?" Bella asked, changing the subject. She got three nods in return. The girls piled their bags out of the way in the living room and dashed up the stairs after Bella.

In Bella's room, Ivy claimed the window seat, curling her legs beneath her. Clara plopped into Bella's brown-and-pink polka-dot beanbag chair. She pushed it next to Bella's bed and sank back into the cozy chair. Violet and Bella sat down on Bella's pink couch.

Just smile, breathe, and don't *get upset. They thought you were sick. They* had *to go today.* Bella turned on the big TV screen and scrolled through her list of recorded shows.

"Ooh, wait a sec!" Clara said. "We need to explain the party to Violet. Can we do that and then start a show?"

Bella and Ivy nodded. This time, Bella really did want to tell her cousin all about Friday's party.

"Yes, let's!" Ivy said.

"Clara, you start," Bella said.

Clara grinned. She did a little dance in her seat. "Violet, you already know that Ivy and I go to school here with Bella, right?"

"Yes," Violet said. "Doesn't your dad work here, Ivy?"

"He is a groundskeeper for the castle," Ivy explained. "I brought Clara to the castle with me one day because I just knew that she and Bella would get along."

"The three of us totally clicked," Bella said. "We were best friends so fast. My mom and dad saw how happy I was once I'd made friends with Ivy and Clara. That's when they got the idea to invite other kids to have school in the castle."

"But I'm the odd one," Clara said, giggling. "My parents work in town at Crystal Bank and Crystal Kingdom Inn. I sneaked in because of Ivy."

They all laughed.

"Ooh, that's right. Your parents don't work here," Bella said, teasing Clara. "I'm kicking you out of our classroom!"

Clara stuck out her tongue at Bella.

Grinning, Ivy rolled her eyes. "So we have

seven other people in our class, including Ben. He's a little older than us, so our tutor, Ms. Barnes, gives him higher-level work. The other six kids are our age—eight."

"My parents didn't even tell *me* about the party," Bella said. "Ivy, Clara, and I all found out at the same time. Ms. Barnes said that we got the entire week off and on Friday, the class was invited to come to the castle." She took one sip of soda and then another.

"Ms. Barnes didn't get *super* specific," Clara added. "All we know is there will be a movie, music, and desserts."

"Oh! Add a giant wooden platform to that list," Bella said. "I watched some construction workers this morning. It looks like they're building a dance floor or something."

Violet's eyes widened. "I would be way too nervous to dance in front of your class. I don't know any of them."

"You know Ben," Ivy said. "Everyone in our class is friendly. You'll fit right in."

"Totally," Clara said. "I wish you could go to school with us! Wouldn't that be the best, Bella?"

"The best," Bella echoed, her tone a little flat.

"Bells," Violet said, "is it okay if I go get us some snacks?"

"Sure," the princess replied. "Use my intercom if you want to reach the kitchen staff."

But Violet stood. "That's okay! I'll just run down there and be right back."

"Ooh, I want to pick out snacks!" Clara thrust up her hand for Violet to grab.

"Me too!" Ivy jumped up. "Be right back!" she said over her shoulder to Bella.

Giggling, the girls ran out of the room and down the hallway, leaving Bella sitting alone in her room.

"Ugh," Bella said aloud. She pulled the purple pillow from under her head and placed it over her face. The princess squeezed her eyes shut and tried to block all the *Violet! Violet! Violet! Violet!* thoughts that wouldn't quiet down in her head. Suddenly Friday felt *very* far away.

5

Stable, Dinner, Sleep, Repeat

As the Friday class party got closer, Bella felt as if she and Violet were growing further and further apart.

The same routine played out every day since Violet's first day at Crystal Castle. Violet always managed to be up before Bella. The princess had even set an alarm so she would wake earlier, but over the past four mornings, this one included, Violet had been awake and dressed, and had either eaten breakfast or been in the process of eating when Bella had reached the kitchen.

Every time Bella asked Violet what she wanted

to do, Violet had the same answer: Go to the royal stables and visit Glimmer. Not that Bella *ever* wanted to stay away from Glimmer, but she was starting to feel as though Glimmer was Violet's unicorn and not hers.

Ben always helped Violet groom or feed Glimmer when Bella's cousin came to the stable without Bella.

And, as if that wasn't enough, Ivy and Clara *adored* Violet. Bella had started to come up with more excuses not to hang with the three girls because she felt like an outsider with her own best friends. She didn't know what her cousin was up to at the moment. Actually, she hadn't seen Violet for a couple of hours.

"Five more minutes," Bella said to Glimmer.

Bella had taken Glimmer from her stall and released her into one of the castle's grassy pastures. Gentle sunlight beamed down on them, and it was a cloudless day in Crystal Kingdom. A light, warm breeze blew back Glimmer's mane as the white unicorn nibbled on grass. Bella wanted—no, *needed*—to talk to someone, so she had taken Glimmer outside where no one was around to hear her talk. She was sitting in the pasture, knees drawn up to her chest.

"The very last thing I want to tell you is about yesterday morning," Bella said. "I got up and, of course, Violet was already up. I went into the back room of the castle that leads to one of the patios."

Glimmer took a step closer to Bella and munched the long green stalks of grass.

"I peered through the glass, and Violet was sitting in a lawn chair, using her Chat Crystal. I blinked, like, fifty times to make sure what I was seeing was real."

Glimmer's big brown eyes stared into Bella's as the unicorn listened.

"Violet was talking to *Clara*. As in, *my* best friend Clara. Without me!" Bella let out a giant sigh and ripped up the stalks of grass that she had been twisting around her fingers.

"I'm so confused, Glimmer. Before Violet got here, all I wanted was for her to make friends with Ivy and Clara and for you to bond with her. All that has happened, and it's not what I was expecting, I guess. I feel like somebody crashing their party."

Glimmer cocked her head as she looked at Bella.

"They haven't really left me out of anything, but I don't think they'd miss me."

It was true—all of the girls had taken a carriage ride through the Crystal Kingdom countryside, played hide-and-seek in the lush gardens, and spent hours petting all the royal unicorns. But Bella could barely get in a sentence among Ivy, Clara, and Violet.

"Bye, Glimmer," Bella said, hugging her unicorn. "I'm going to find Violet." She kissed Glimmer's check and went back to the castle.

Violet's room was empty, so Bella went back to her own room. She climbed onto the window seat and pulled out her Chat Crystal.

Bella desperately wanted to talk to Lyssa, but her older friend had the week off, and she didn't want to call Lyssa on her break and bother her. Bella had thought about talking to her mom, but her mom loved Violet and just wouldn't understand.

The class party was two days away. Some of Bella's classmates had sent her messages, saying how excited they were about Friday. Queen Katherine and King Phillip had spent hours each day working on different aspects of the party—most of which were kept secret from Bella.

The princess had thought that the class party would be practically the only thing Violet, Ivy, and Clara would want to talk about. That and Violet's upcoming ceremony. Bella had brought those up in conversation every day up until this morning, and her besties and cousin weren't nearly as into it as Bella had imagined. Violet, especially. She shut down *any* talk about the Pairing Ceremony. Bella didn't even bother to try to talk to her cousin about it anymore. The only topic that seemed to hold Violet's attention was unicorns. And more unicorns.

And *more* unicorns. It was almost like Violet was skipping over the ceremony in her head and going straight to the unicorn part.

Talking about unicorns was *far* from boring for Bella. But Violet was so bubbly every time they talked—and she seemed to only want to discuss the awesome parts of having a unicorn. No mentions of the birthday ceremony, fear about not finding Violet's perfect match—anything! Bella couldn't believe that Violet hadn't come to her yet with questions about the Pairing Ceremony.

But, despite Violet's always cheery attitude, Bella made a promise to herself that she would find the right time to sit Violet down and explain all about red auras and Queen Fire's presence in her life. She didn't want to rain on her cousin's Pairing Ceremony, but she did want Violet to be prepared for anything.

Bella, sitting with her legs stretched in front of her, looked out her window at the party preparations. Queen Katherine stood in the center of the now-finished wooden stage, gesturing as she talked to one of the party planners. Tiny pinpricks of excitement covered Bella's arms. Her first-*ever* school party! It would have been a little scary if Bella's class was huge and if she didn't know everyone. But all of her classmates knew each other—and were all friends.

Bella tried to put herself in Violet's place. *I would feel nervous,* she thought. *Meeting new people is always a little scary. But she knows Ivy, Clara, and me.*

Bella still didn't understand why Ivy and Clara suddenly didn't seem excited about Friday anymore. BV (Before Violet) the princess's besties hadn't stopped talking about the party. Now, AV (After Violet) it was only a topic of conversation if Bella brought it up.

Bella rubbed her eyes. Nothing about this vacation was going as she had imagined. Not as though it had been bad or anything, but it was weird somehow, in some way Bella couldn't quite put her finger on.

She sighed. Ivy and Clara were going to be at Crystal Castle in a few hours. They'd planned a sleepover tonight. Each girl was supposed to bring a different color nail polish. Bella had so many bottles of Sunray Sweets polishes in reds, pinks, purples—even a yellow one! The best part of a mani-pedi was after the color and applying a coat of Sunray Sweets Shine-On top coat. The polish, packed with sunray berries, glowed when it was applied. As it dried, the polish began to shine brighter and brighter. Nails looked as if they had their own tiny spotlight. The polish's glow turned off at night and recharged when back in the sun.

Bella stretched and stood. It was just after noon. Maybe Violet was in her room now. It had been at least half an hour since Bella had last checked. *You need to stop acting like you're five and just call Ivy and Clara,* Bella told herself. *They're not mind readers. How can they know something's wrong if you don't tell them?*

Bella walked down the hall, slowing when she heard Vi's voice.

Bella tiptoed to her cousin's door and leaned toward the cracked opening.

". . . Dad, really! Glimmer is . . . wish . . ."

Bella stepped away from the door. If Violet's conversation with her dad were anything like the ones she had with Bella and her friends, Violet was going to be on the phone for a while.

Bella picked up her Chat Crystal. Suddenly she needed to talk to Ivy and Clara more than anything.

Bella placed the round crystal flat on her palm. She stared at it. "Ivy, Clara, can I call you?" She paused. "Send message, please."

The crystal blinked its silver I'M WORKING ON IT message.

While she waited to hear back from her friends, Bella sifted through some of the outfits she had narrowed down for the party. *I wish I knew what my friends were thinking of wearing*, she thought. *We could be choosing our clothes together.*

Bella shut the closet door. Hard. She reached for the clear Chat Crystal, and it blinked purple and pink the second her fingertips touched it.

Ivy and Clara were able to talk. Bella ran honey gloss over her lips, trying to decide how to approach her friends with her feelings about Violet.

Both of the princess's friends seemed to have gotten close to Violet. Fast. Bella looked up at the photographs of her and her friends that practically covered the wall space above her desk.

She placed her Chat Crystal on a cloud-shaped pillow in front of her. "Please call Ivy and Clara," Bella commanded. A bright silver flash, then beams of pink light fanned in front of Bella. Purple shot up next to the pink so the colors were side by side. This was a new feature designers had recently added to the Chat Crystals.

The colors faded as images of Ivy and Clara appeared in their places. Ivy, cross-legged in her desk chair, waved at Bella before turning her head in Clara's direction. Ivy smiled at Clara, who did the same and, teasingly, stuck out her tongue at Bella.

"What's up, Princess?" Clara asked. "Or, excuse me. Let me try again. What matter do you, erm, wish to talk—no, *speak*—of, Your Highness?"

Ivy and Clara giggled, but they stopped short when they saw Bella's serious expression. Both girls sat up a little straighter, and Ivy clutched her hands in her lap.

The princess chewed on the inside of her cheek. "Something's kind of bothering me. You guys are going to think I'm being dumb," she said.

"Don't say that," Ivy said. "We've never said that and we never would."

Clara bobbed her head in agreement. "Exactly. Bella, we're your best friends. Nothing that's upsetting you is *ever* going to be small or dumb to us."

Bella gave her friends a tiny smile. She took a deep breath. "This is really hard for me to say, but I want to be honest with you because you're my best friends. It feels like you guys and Violet became friends so fast. Which I'm *happy about*." Bella added the last sentence really fast. "I love that my favorite cousin and my favorite friends like each other so much. I just feel left out. Like you guys wouldn't notice if I wasn't there."

"What are you talking about?" Ivy said. "We would *so* notice if you weren't with us. Bella, if you think we're being extra nice or something to Violet, it's because she's your cousin."

"Ivy's right," Clara said. "I was kind of nervous about Violet visiting, because I really wanted to like her and get along with her because of how close you guys are. Ivy and I are your best friends! We'd never, ever want to hurt your feelings. You and Ivy are so important to me—like family!"

"We didn't choose Violet over you," Ivy added. "I was only trying to be nice to your cousin—I promise. I'm so sorry you felt left out."

"Me too," Clara said. "Maybe Ivy and I sort of treated Violet like a shiny new toy. I'm sorry I made you feel like you weren't included, Bella."

The knots in Bella's stomach loosened a little.

"Thank you both for saying what you did," the princess said. "I—I also wanted to talk to you without Violet around to see if you were still as excited about the class party as you were before Violet got here."

"Are you kidding?" Ivy asked. "I get more excited every day!"

"Me too!" Clara said, smiling at Ivy and then at Bella.

"But we're not talking about it. Ever," Bella said. "I've tried to bring it up, and the conversation always goes back to unicorns."

"Violet seems more comfortable talking about stuff other than the party," Clara said. She shrugged. "Maybe she's a little nervous?"

"I don't know," Bella said.

"Have you talked to Violet about this?" Ivy asked.

"Not yet," Bella said. "I wanted to talk to each of you first."

"What do you guys talk about when Ivy and I aren't there?" Clara asked. "Have you talked to her about your Pairing Ceremony and Queen Fire?"

Bella shook her head so hard it almost made her dizzy. "Violet's being so annoying!" she complained. "I barely see her. If I do, she's always at the stable with Glimmer. We haven't talked for one second about my ceremony. I thought she would want to know more, since her ceremony is soon."

"It sounds like you two need to sit down and talk," Ivy said. "You've got to tell Violet how you feel."

"I feel like Violet wants to steal Glimmer or something," Bella said, only half joking. "She must think that her Pairing Ceremony is going to be so perfect that she doesn't need any advice from her cousin. She hadn't been acting like the Violet that I remembered."

"Definitely talk to her," Clara said. "Sooner rather than later."

"Okay," Bella said. "I'll go see if she's done talking to Dad. Thanks for putting up with me, guys."

The friends blew kisses to each other, and Ivy and Clara signed off.

Bella put the Chat Crystal beside her bed and went back to the guest room. Once again, she leaned close to the door. Silence.

"Violet?" Bella called, knocking on the door. "You still on the phone?"

After a few seconds with no response, Bella opened the door. The guest room was empty. She went back to her room and pulled on boots. At least she knew where to find Violet: the stable.

6

Glimmer's Gone Green

Minutes later Bella reached the stable. Ben wasn't in front of Glimmer's stall like he had been so often over the past few days. *Maybe they're inside the stall with Glimmer,* she thought. She could see the stall door was bolted tight.

"Violet? Ben?" Bella said, reaching Glimmer's stall. "Are you—"

She stopped midsentence.

"Ben! HELP!" Bella yelled. "Frederick! Help! Please!"

Her fingers felt clumsy as she unbolted the stall door and stepped in. She blinked furiously.

Gone were any traces of Glimmer's usual purple color. Instead Bella's unicorn was a vibrant emerald green from nose to tail!

Oh NO!

"Bella?" Ben called down the stable aisle.

"In Glimmer's stall!" Bella yelled back. "Glimmer's sick!"

The princess reached a hand out to Glimmer's cheek. Glimmer didn't feel hot.

Ben skidded to a stop and entered the stall. Immediately he began feeling Glimmer's muzzle, looking into her eyes and ears, and lifting up her lip.

"What's wrong with her?" Bella said, trying not to cry. If she cried, she would probably scare Glimmer.

"Glimmer, tell me what's wrong," she said.

"Bella."

Bella turned at the sound of her father's voice.

King Phillip stood outside Glimmer's stall with Frederick.

"Ben," Frederick said. "Come."

Ben bowed his head to King Phillip and did as he was told. The king nodded at Ben.

"Dad, we need Frederick!" Bella said. "Where is he going?"

"He's going to explain to Ben why Glimmer changed color," her dad said. "Glimmer isn't sick, sweetie."

"She's not?" Bella's knees almost crumpled under her from relief. "Then what's wrong?"

"Let's take a walk together," King Phillip said. He held out a hand to Bella. She took her dad's warm hand and stepped out of the stall. She latched Glimmer's stall door and followed her dad out of the stable.

Sunlight beamed down on them and made the castle seal on King Phillip's shirt sparkle. He turned his kind green eyes to Bella. "How have things been going with Violet?" the king asked.

Bella looked up at her dad. "Good," she said. Then she frowned. "Okay, not so great. But Dad, what's wrong with Glimmer?"

"Glimmer will be just fine," King Phillip said. "Tell me what's going on." He and Bella started down a pebble-lined path to one of the ponds. Bella wanted to know right now why her beautiful, sweet unicorn was green, but it seemed like her dad wouldn't tell her without Bella answering his question.

"I guess things aren't going exactly as I expected," Bella said. "I was feeling a little left out because Violet, Ivy, and Clara became friends like that." She snapped her fingers. "Plus, Glimmer loved Violet from the moment they met. I promise, Dad, I'm so happy that everyone likes Violet so much. That's why it's so confusing, I guess, that I keep having these weird moments of being annoyed at her."

The king nodded. "Have you told Violet any of this?"

"Not yet," Bella said. "I talked to Ivy and Clara before I came to the stable. I told them how I felt, and they understood. They told me I should talk to Violet, and I was looking for her at the stable."

The princess and her father walked the rest of the way down the path in silence and reached a wooden dock. Bella walked to the far end and sat down, swinging her legs above the water. King Phillip sat beside her. The water turned clear as Bella glanced at the pond. When Bella was little, she always wished she could see the creatures at the bottom of the pond, so King Phillip had applied a crystal clear spell to the water. Whenever Bella visited and glanced at the water, it would become crystal clear and the princess would be able to see the life at the bottom of the pond.

A small boat tied to the dock bobbed in the water. It had a glass bottom so Bella could watch crabs, fish, and other creatures whenever she floated around in the boat.

"There's more," King Phillip said. "I can tell. I happen to know my daughter very well." The king touched Bella's arm with his hand. "What else is wrong, Bells? You can always talk to me."

"I know I can," the princess said. "It's hard. I don't know what I'm feeling! This whole week was supposed to be about the party on Friday. But all Violet wants to talk about is unicorns, and she hasn't even asked me how my ceremony went. Every time I bring it up, she doesn't want to talk about it. It's like she thinks her Pairing Ceremony is going to be easy and perfect. Or maybe she thinks the ceremony part will be boring. I don't know."

King Phillip reached over and put an arm across Bella's shoulders. Bella leaned against her dad, feeling relieved to have told him what had been going on all week.

"You and Glimmer share a bond that no one else has with you," King Phillip explained. "She is very in tune with all of your emotions and feelings. Glimmer is green, Bella, because you are feeling one emotion *very* strongly."

Bella sat up so she could look at her dad's face. "What? *I* turned Glimmer green?"

"Your feeling of envy or jealousy toward Violet," King Phillip said.

Bella was quiet for a moment. "That's the weird feeling I've had. The thing I didn't know how to explain. It was jealousy all along."

"Jealousy is a powerful emotion," King Phillip explained. "It can motivate people to do things they otherwise wouldn't, make them feel things that possibly aren't true, and it can be a consuming emotion."

"I've been jealous of Violet this whole time," Bella said. "Dad, I was jealous that she and Ivy and

Clara became friends so fast. Same with her and Glimmer. I guess I'm a little hurt, too, that Violet's here and I could have told her every detail about my ceremony, but she doesn't want to hear it."

The king stayed quiet, nodding and listening to his daughter.

"Dad, how do I get Glimmer back to normal?"

The king smiled. "You might want to start with talking to Violet."

Bella wrapped her arms around her dad. The king hugged her back. "I love you, sweetheart," her dad said. "I know you'll have Glimmer back to purple in no time."

Bella scrambled to her feet. "I've got to find Violet right now!"

7

Let's Talk

Almost an hour had passed since Bella had talked to her dad. She still hadn't found Violet. The princess had looked everywhere and asked everyone, but no one had seen her cousin.

Bella finally went back to the castle, deciding to look for Violet inside.

She entered through a side door in the kitchen and almost smacked right into Violet.

"I've been looking everywhere for you!" Bella said. She looked at her cousin. Violet's eyes were pink and her nose was red. "Have you been crying? What's wrong?"

Bella reached out a hand toward Violet, but her cousin yanked her arm away from Bella. "You don't have to be nice," Violet said softly, her chin wobbly as she talked. "I heard you talking to Ivy and Clara. I'm sorry I ruined your entire week. I'm going upstairs to pack and am going home tonight."

Violet turned away from Bella and darted out of the kitchen.

"Violet! Wait!" Bella called after her. But Violet didn't stop. Bella followed her to the guest bedroom and watched as Violet yanked her suitcase on top of the bed and began pulling clothes off hangers and tossing them into the suitcase.

"Violet, please," Bella said. "Please just let me explain. Give me ten minutes, and if you still want to leave after, then I'll help you pack. Okay?"

Violet swiped at her nose with her hand. She plopped on the bed, hanger in hand. "Ten minutes. Go."

"I am so sorry you heard me talking to Ivy and Clara," Bella apologized. "I should have talked to you first. Have you seen Glimmer this afternoon?"

Violet glared at her. "No. I didn't go anywhere near the stable, since I'm trying to steal your unicorn, apparently."

"I'm sorry that I said that, too," Bella said. "But if you had seen Glimmer, you would have been pretty surprised. Because of me being so jealous of you, Glimmer turned green!"

Violet blinked. "She's *green*?"

Bella nodded. "It's all my fault. Glimmer won't go back to normal until I stop feeling so jealous of you."

"Jealous of what?" Violet asked.

So Violet hadn't heard that part of the conversation with Ivy and Clara.

"I'm . . ." Bella paused, taking a deep breath.

"I'm jealous that you got here and everyone instantly wanted to be your friend. Ivy and Clara never make a new friend this fast. You and Ben can talk about Foris all the time. Even Glimmer loves you like crazy!"

Bella took a breath.

"There's just one more thing," the princess

said. "I'm not sure why, but you don't want to talk about the Pairing Ceremony. Ever. I've tried to talk to you about it, and you always stop me. Vi, I was so scared before my ceremony. If you had already done yours, I would have asked you a million questions. You haven't asked me any. It hurt my feelings, too, because my ceremony was the biggest night of my life, and you don't want to hear about it in person."

Bella watched as Violet dropped her head.

"I haven't asked you because it reminds me too much of home," Violet said in a whisper. "Once I go back, it's all that I'll hear about or have to think about. I've been having so much fun with you, Ben, Ivy, and Clara. I don't have one friend at home."

"Oh, Violet," Bella said. Her cousin's lower lip trembled.

"It's so amazing being around friends! On the train ride here I was so scared that I wouldn't fit in and that your friends would think I was weird or something. But they've been so nice. Friday's party is coming up so fast—I don't want this visit to end."

"My friends are the best," Bella agreed. "And there's nothing 'weird' about you, Violet. You'll have to come over more often to be around us. Maybe your parents would consider letting kids of castle employees go to school with you or something."

Violet gave Bella a tiny smile. "That sounds cool and scary at the same time. I feel so lucky to already have made friends here with your help. I'd be really scared to have kids I don't know in a room at my castle."

"They would love you," Bella promised. "Really, Vi. You'd make friends at home just as fast as you did here."

"I'm sorry, Bella," Violet said. "I came here to

be on vacation with you. I was so excited to have *your* friends like *me*. You kind of have to like me because we're family."

"I was jealous because it seemed like all of my friends liked you better than me," Bella replied. "And I didn't feel like we were spending enough cousin time together. I've missed you!"

"I missed you, too!"

Bella pointed at Violet's suitcase. "Ten minutes are probably up. Do you want help packing?"

Violet nodded. "Yes."

Bella felt as though her heart plummeted to her feet.

"With unpacking," Violet said, smiling.

"Ahhh! You totally scared me!" Bella said with a laugh. "Are we okay?"

"More than okay," Violet said. "I know that you, Ivy, and Clara will be at the party. It's not going to be as scary as I thought."

"It's going to be way more fun than you can imagine," Bella said. "Trust me."

"Bella, I would really love to hear about your ceremony, if you still want to tell me about it," Violet said. "Being scared of my own ceremony was the reason I spent so much time with Glimmer. I thought if I spent time with a happily matched unicorn that it would help me somehow at my ceremony. I'm sorry that I kind of treated Glimmer like my own unicorn."

"It's okay," Bella said. "I understand now. Of course I'll tell you about my ceremony. There's so much you don't know. And after that, maybe we can pick outfits for the party?"

Violet nodded. "I'd like that. I definitely need help choosing the perfect outfit."

"Me too. That's why I'm glad you're here. Sparkling grape juice toast please," Bella declared. "Hold your hand like mine," she told Violet.

A glass appeared in each of their hands. Bubbly grape juice filled each of their glasses.

"Too cool," Violet said, grinning. "So remembering that trick at home."

Bella raised her glass. "Here's to starting over, to being good best friends, and being the best cousins ever!"

"Yay to that!" Ivy grinned.

The girls clinked their glasses together, then took a sip of their juice. They finished their small glasses quickly.

After a final squeeze, they left the guest room and headed for the stables.

Crossing her fingers for luck, Bella peered into Glimmer's stall.

Purple!

Glimmer let out a soft whine and walked up to the stall door. She nuzzled Bella and Violet.

"Oh, Glimmer!" Bella exclaimed. "I'm so glad

you're purple again! I promise never to let that happen again."

"Let's talk inside her stall," Bella said to Violet. The girls went into the stall and sat down on clean straw. Glimmer circled once, then lowered herself onto the straw next to the girls.

"So," Bella started, "there's a *lot* that happened at my ceremony. Some of it is amazing and some of it not so much."

"I want to hear all of it," Violet said.

And so Bella told Violet all about her ceremony, red auras, Queen Fire's scary appearance on Bella's birthday, and details about the nasty, evil queen of the Blacklands.

The cousins talked for hours—so long that Glimmer fell asleep. By the end of the conversation, Violet was super excited for her own ceremony—exactly what Bella had hoped for. The girls decided not to spend another second talking about Queen Fire, and instead they left a sleeping Glimmer in her stall and headed up to the castle. Lightning bugs flashed across the castle property—the girls had talked until the sun had started to set.

That night Bella went to bed in a better mood than she had been in all week. The girls stayed up talking and giggling, just like Bella had always wanted for the visit. Bella drifted off to sleep, glad to have her cousin by her side, and vowing to make sure the rest of Violet's visit was magical.

8

Lyssa to the Rescue

Bella blinked, staring up at her ceiling. An excited tingle ran through her body. She looked at her clock. Just after nine in the morning.

"Violet," Bella whispered. Her cousin was sound asleep next to her, clutching one of Bella's stuffed unicorns.

"Violet!" Bella said, louder this time. "It's party day!"

Violet turned on her side, facing Bella. Strands of red hair had escaped from the French braid she had done last night.

"Oh! It's Friday!" Violet sat up, hugging the

unicorn. "Omigosh! I'm so nervous and excited at the same time!"

Bella grinned. "No nerves necessary! You know four people already—Ben, Ivy, Clara, and me. You won't be alone for a second. Let's go have breakfast!"

They both climbed out of Bella's bed and put on matching fluffy light-blue cotton robes. Thursday had passed in a blur. Ivy and Clara had come over, and everyone had done mani pedis. The girls pooled their collections of Sunray Sweets nail polishes.

"You said Lyssa is coming today, right?" Violet asked as the cousins walked down the hallway together.

"Yes. She might even be here now. I asked her to help get our outfits ready."

"Ooh, I can't wait to meet her," Violet said.

The girls reached the breakfast table, and

Bella's parents stood to hug each of the girls.

"How did you sleep?" Queen Katherine asked. She raised an eyebrow at Bella. "You *did* sleep a little, right?"

"We did, Aunt Katherine," Violet said. "I fell asleep instantly."

"Me too," Bella added. "I thought I'd be awake all night thinking about the party, but I think my body knew I needed to rest up for today."

Queen Katherine smiled. "Good girls," she said. She and King Phillip remained standing as Bella and Violet sat in front of empty plates.

"We have a few last-minute details to attend to," Queen Katherine said. "Enjoy your breakfast."

Violet and Bella smiled as the king and queen left the dining room. Silver trays reached from one end of the table to another. The clear lids revealed eggs, pancakes, sausages, bacon—so many yummy options!

Bella and Violet filled their plates, and Bella was on her last chocolate chip pancake when she heard footsteps behind her.

"Morning!" a cheery voice called.

"Lyssa!" Bella said. "I'm so happy you're here! Thank you for coming. Violet, this is Lyssa."

"I've heard so much about you from Bella," Lyssa said, smiling at Violet. "I'm so glad to finally meet you."

"Me too," Violet said. "Bella said you can put together perfect party outfits. I so need your help!"

Lyssa grinned. "Aw, I'm glad Bella says nice things about me. She usually tells everyone how I mismatch her socks and try to dress her in stripes and polka dots at the same time."

Bella dropped her jaw. "I do not!"

Lyssa winked at her, and all three girls burst into laughter. Bella said a silent *thank you* for Lyssa being there. The older girl was sure to help Bella and Violet look amazing and help with Violet's nerves, too.

"It's my pleasure to come over," Lyssa said cheerfully. "I stopped by yesterday, too."

"You did?" Bella asked. "I didn't even see you."

Lyssa smiled. "I peeked in on you two and Ivy and Clara. You were *very* serious about the right nail polish." Everyone laughed.

"I'm finished with breakfast if you are," Bella said to Violet. Her cousin nodded.

"Then let the party makeovers begin, ladies!" Lyssa said.

Bella and Violet clapped. Giggling, the three of them headed upstairs.

"Even though the party is, like, eight hours away, I feel like I won't be ready in time," Bella said.

"We have *plenty* of time," Lyssa assured her.

"We're going to do hair and face masks and a little spa time before we really start getting ready."

In Bella's room, Lyssa pulled the dresses she had selected the day before. She spread the four choices across the bed.

"Did you bring dresses for tonight?" Lyssa asked Violet.

"They're in the guest room," Violet said. "I brought a few and went shopping here. It would be so great if you helped me choose."

"Of course," Lyssa said. "All right. Bella, hop in the shower and wash your hair. While you're showering, I'm going to help Violet settle on a dress. Then Violet, you'll shower while I help Bella. Then I'll do hair masks for deep conditioning, okay?"

"Yes!" Bella and Violet chorused.

Violet grinned at Bella. Seeing her cousin smile like that made Bella even more excited for tonight. It was going to be the best party ever!

9

Social Butterfly

Lyssa had just finished curling Bella's hair when Ivy and Clara, both in Crystal Castle carriages, arrived. Each classmate of theirs was being picked up by a carriage.

"Wow!" Clara said, stepping back to look at Bella and Violet. "You both look amazing!"

Bella blushed and saw color flushing Violet's cheeks too.

"Lyssa helped us pick out the outfits," Bella said. "She was with us all morning and afternoon."

Bella wore a teal scoop-neck dress with a tulle skirt covered in petal appliqués. The dress had a bow at her right hip, and it zipped up the back. Bella's feet were comfy in black peep-toe ballet flats. Lyssa had curled Bella's naturally straight brown hair, and it fell in waves around her shoulders.

Violet sparkled in a hunter-green dress. The color made her red hair pop. The dress had three layers of ruffles along the bottom, and it was dotted with light-catching green sequins. Violet wore a pair of Bella's rhinestone-dotted black velvet ballet flats. Lyssa had flat-ironed Violet's curls into straight, shiny curtains of red hair.

Violet and Bella had hugged Lyssa and thanked her over and over as they left Bella's room. Once outside, the girls followed a smooth path that had been placed over the grass and led to the stage. Each time Bella put a foot on the path, it changed colors.

A carriage came to a smooth stop in the driveway and Todd, a boy in Bella's class, jumped out of the carriage. Todd followed the light-path and climbed the stairs to the platform.

"Hey," he said to the girls. He had bright-green eyes and freckles sprinkled across his nose.

"Hey, Todd," Bella said. "This is my cousin, Violet."

Todd smiled. "Hi."

Bella leaned close to Violet. "See? It's not so bad, right?"

Violet nodded. "I think this is going to be fun!"

Upbeat music played through big music crystals that rotated around the platform. The sun was just about to set, and rainbow-colored spot-lights flickered on and off.

More carriages arrived, and each time, Bella made sure to introduce Violet until she had met each person in Bella's class.

"Ben!" Bella stuck her arm in the air and waved

at the dark-haired boy who stood on the platform's edge. Clara, next to Bella, waved at Ben too.

Smiling, Ben nodded at the other people, who were in groups chatting and swaying to the music.

"You look nice," Bella said to Ben. Ben had on a black shirt with black pants instead of his usual stable uniform.

"Thanks. You all look nice too," Ben said. "This is going to be fun! It was so nice of your parents to do this."

"I know. We all see each other every day, but really never get a chance to hang out," Bella said. "Tonight we can!"

"May I have your attention, everyone?"

All the kids turned their heads in the direction of the front of the stage. Queen Katherine, in a sunny yellow dress, smiled at them from atop a small podium.

"I'm so excited to have all of Bella's classmates

here tonight," Queen Katherine said. "A party was long overdue! I read progress reports for each of you and know how hard you work at school. I'm so proud to have you as students at Crystal Castle."

Everyone started clapping.

"There are some yummy treats under the red tent," Queen Katherine said once the applause died down. "The party ends at nine, but if you would like to go home sooner, come find me or King Phillip and we'll get a carriage ready. This isn't the last party, by the way. I am already planning an end-of-spring party, and I hope you'll all come!"

Cheers rang out across the platform.

"Thank you, Queen Katherine!" Todd shouted from his spot next to Bella.

"Thank you!" the rest of the class added.

"You're welcome, and have fun!" the queen said.

Music began flowing through the speakers again. Bella almost hopped up and down when she glanced around and spotted Violet chatting away with a few kids from the class.

Bella, Ivy, Clara, and Ben started dancing and talking as they moved around the floor. The platform lit up under their feet just as the walkway had done.

No one was on the sidelines—every person in Bella's class was dancing on the floor. "Are you having fun?" Bella asked Violet as she sidled up next to her cousin.

"So much fun!" Violet threw an arm around Bella. "Thank you for inviting me! This is one of the best nights ever!"

"Aw, I'm so glad!" Bella said, hugging her cousin back.

Bella accepted an empty plastic cup from Ben and peered at the bottom. "Sunray and cranberry juice with ice, please," she said. Immediately two ice cubes appeared in her cup, and it slowly filled with orange-red liquid until it was just full enough. Bella took one sip and then another. Sunray juice was so good! It was sour and sweet and unlike any other fruit in Crystal Kingdom.

Ben and Bella chatted about Glimmer's green transformation.

"Uncle Frederick explained it to me," Ben said. "That's so amazing, Bella. I can't even imagine having a unicorn so in tune with me that she changes colors if I'm feeling something so strong."

"In this case, it was kind of a curse," Bella said, shaking her head. "But I hope if Glimmer ever changes colors again that it will be from a good emotion that I'm having."

"Hey," Ben said, touching Bella's arm. "No one's perfect. You must have worked it out, because the last time I saw Glimmer, she was purple."

"I had a little help from my dad," Bella said. "I finally did the right thing and I learned my lesson."

After dancing for a while, everyone headed to the Bamboo Garden. A giant movie screen appeared in the air as the students plopped down onto lounge chairs, blankets spread on the soft ground. During the movie, trays with dozens of delicious desserts floated to everyone. At the end of the movie, the credits rolled and the music began again.

Soon the sun had set, but everyone was going strong. Violet, a new social butterfly, flitted from group to group, and Bella couldn't help but grin as she watched her cousin. Violet and Adrienne, a cheery girl in a tangerine-colored dress, were off to the side of the floor talking.

The party was perfect. Bella couldn't have asked for anything more. She hoped that Violet would go home with new friends and maybe convince her parents to invite kids of Foris's castle workers to school at the castle.

"Bella," Ivy called out, almost having to shout to be heard over the music. "Some lady in a Crystal Castle uniform wants to talk to you. I feel like I've seen her before, but I don't know why."

"I bet she's one of the party planners. She probably can't find my mom or dad," Bella said.

"She said she would be waiting for you by the food tent," Ivy said.

"Thanks, Ivy," Bella said. "Be right back."

Bella hurried down the platform steps and peered inside the massive tent. The red canvas covered the banquet tables full of food and drinks.

"Hello?" Bella called.

"Over here," a pleasant voice replied. Bella spotted a blond woman waving and smiling.

Bella walked over to the woman. "If you're looking for my parents, they're around here somewhere," Bella said.

"Oh, no, dear," the woman said. Her blond hair started turning black at the roots, and her rosy cheeks paled. Ruby-red lips and eyes that glittered black stared at Bella.

"I'm not looking for your parents." The woman continued to change in front of Bella's eyes. The princess gulped. Goose bumps covered her arms. It felt as though the temperature had dropped fifty degrees!

Black hair cascaded down the woman's back, and the ends were red. The Crystal Castle uniform was replaced with a black cape and a long black dress that touched the ground.

The sweetness was gone from the woman's voice. A hard edge with a rough tone was in its place.

"I'm looking for *you*."

Queen Fire was here.

10

IOU

"What are you doing?" Bella asked the evil queen, heart thumping. "My father forbid you from ever setting food on our land again. The second guards see you, they'll take you right to a jail cell."

Even as she said the words, Bella knew that she couldn't call security. If she did, Queen Fire would certainly tell Bella's parents about their encounter in the Dark Forest. The king and queen would be beyond furious if they ever learned of Bella's trip onto the forbidden land.

Queen Fire laughed. It was an eerie cackle that sent shivers down Bella's spine. Bella glanced around, worried that someone might have heard, but the tent was empty. Everyone was dancing onstage or talking on the sidelines. Bella was grateful that none of them were near Queen Fire. She hated that her aunt had just spoken to Ivy.

"No one can see or hear us," Queen Fire said. "See the black ring?" She nodded toward the ground. There was a circle of black powder around them.

"What is it?" Bella asked.

"Just a little privacy wall spell," the queen said. "I would have hated for security to come. I know my dear twin sister doesn't want to see me. Pity that I must cast a spell to be allowed to speak to my niece."

Queen Fire had Bella cornered and she knew it. Bella clenched her hands into fists, willing herself to stay calm. "You did this to yourself," Bella said. "It's not my parents' fault that you aren't part of our family."

"Oh, Bella," Queen Fire said. "You have so much to learn about the truth behind my exile from Crystal Castle. But that is a story for another day. I have another matter that brought me here to speak with you."

Bella's mouth went dry. Her thoughts raced back to that day in the Dark Forest. She knew why Queen Fire was here. The only thing Bella wanted was to make Queen Fire happy so she would leave without anyone ever knowing she had been there.

"I want you to leave," Bella commanded. "This party is important to all of my friends. What do you want?"

The queen smiled at the princess, her lips coated in red lipstick. "I'm here to collect, Bella. You did promise me a favor, after all."

Bella tried to slow her speeding heart rate. "What is it?" She couldn't think of anything the

queen didn't already have or couldn't get on her own.

Queen Fire laughed. She took a step closer to Bella. "No, not money or jewels."

Bella's eyes widened.

Queen Fire pointed an index finger at her. The long nail, painted bloodred, matched her lipstick. "Silly girl. I want *you*."

HERE'S A SNEAK PEEK AT BELLA AND
GLIMMER'S NEXT ADVENTURE:

The Hidden Treasure

Princess Bella stared at her evil aunt, Queen Fire, trying to look brave. Bella had been having a great time with the rest of her classmates at a fun dance that her parents, King Frederick and Queen Katherine, had planned to celebrate the end of the year. But Queen Fire had been a not-so-fun party surprise.

"How long does this"—Bella pointed to the black powder that hid them both from the other guests—"last?"

"Dear niece, don't worry about our privacy," Queen Fire said in a sugar-sweet tone. Bella's aunt had raven-black hair that hung down her back, glittering eyes, and matching ruby-red lips and nails.

"Did you have to come during my party?" Bella asked.

"I can come and go whenever I please," Queen Fire said. She glanced away from Bella, taking in the happy chatter and fun as Bella's classmates danced nearby.

Bella started to say something, but she bit her lip to keep quiet. Had she imagined the flicker of sadness on Queen Fire's face?

"Please let me go," Bella begged. "This is the last day I can spend with my cousin before she goes home. I know I owe you a favor, though, and I am not going back on my promise."

Images flashed through Bella's mind—picture after picture of that horrible time when Glimmer, her unicorn, had run away to the Dark Forest. Bella and Glimmer had just started to get to know each other after Bella had been matched with Glimmer on her eighth birthday. But Glimmer had run away, and when Bella had found her in the scary Dark Forest, they were suddenly in the path of Queen Fire's dangerous unicorns. Bella and Glimmer had been seconds away from serious trouble before Queen Fire saved them. In turn, Bella had pledged to help her aunt if she ever needed. And if she did not help her aunt, her aunt was going to take Glimmer away.

Queen Fire crossed her arms. "I had a feeling you would back out of our deal."

Bella felt like she was underwater—like someone had stuffed cotton balls in her ears. The class party felt very far away, and Bella did not know what to say to her aunt.

"Fine," Queen Fire sighed, waving a pale hand in the air. "Go back to your party, dear. I'm getting rather tired of hiding, though. I want you at *my* castle tomorrow by noon."

Bella chewed on the inside of her cheek. She didn't want to ask more questions that would keep the queen here longer, but . . .

"Can I come on Sunday? Please? Tomorrow is my last day with my cousin before she goes home to Foris."

Queen Fire stared, unblinking, at Bella. "Sunday. Noon. Or I'll have my guards begin to ready a stall at my stables for Glimmer."

"Not a cha—"

Queen Fire vanished before Bella could finish her sentence. Bella looked down, and all the black powder had disappeared too.

Okay, pull yourself together, Bella. You can't let anyone see that you're upset.

Bella glanced down at her shaking hands. She

walked over to a crystal punch bowl floating in the air.

"One cup, please," she said, testing out her voice. She thought she sounded like her usual self.

A ladle dipped into the bowl, filling a cup with red punch. The cup lowered itself in front of Bella.

"Thank you." Bella took the cup and sipped, trying to shake off Queen Fire's visit. She smoothed her sparkly teal dress with her free hand.

"Bella?"

A familiar voice called her name.

"Over here," Bella said as she forced a smile onto her face.

Her best friends, Ivy and Clara, along with her cousin, Violet, surrounded her.

"Did you help that lady who was looking for you?" Ivy asked.

Bella nodded, grabbing Ivy's hand and tugging her forward. "Yes. Let's go back to the party."

The princess accompanied her friends out of the tent and made a silent vow never to let Queen Fire that close to her friends ever again.

Mermaid Tales

Exciting under-the-sea adventures with Shelly and her mermaid friends!

Candy Fairies

Chocolate Dreams	Rainbow Swirl	Caramel Moon	Cool Mint	Magic Hearts	Gooey Goblins

The Sugar Ball	A Valentine's Surprise	Bubble Gum Rescue	Double Dip	Jelly Bean Jumble	The Chocolate Rose

A Royal Wedding	Marshmallow Mystery	Frozen Treats	The Sugar Cup	Sweet Secrets	Taffy Trouble

Visit candyfairies.com
for games, recipes, and more!

Break out your sleeping
bag and best pajamas. . . .
You're invited!

Sleepover Squad

❀ Collect them all! ❀